# Too Many Moose!

Written by
2016
Lisa M Bakos

Illustrated by
2016
Mark Chambers

sourcebooks
jabberwocky

When Martha decided she must have a pet,
she marveled and mulled over what she should get.
But much of the choices made Martha quite glum…
instead of magnificent, most were humdrum.

And just as it seemed like it might be no use…
she made up her mind

that
    she

must

have

one…

FOOD

BEARD

MOOSE DANCE

41

The mailman delivered her new moose midday.

She signed with an M...

and they both marched away.

They shared an umbrella,

they sipped maple tea.

They carved hearts and $\mathcal{M}$s
on a mulberry tree.

They went to the movies;
they shopped at the mall.
They both got a manicure,
polish and all.

"My moose is so marvelous!"
Martha declared.

Not much could match up
when her moose was compared.

So Martha,
    quite merrily,

            ordered

                    one

                            more...

and
one more

and
one more

until she had
**four!**

The mailman delivered her new moose midday.

She signed with an *M*...
and they all marched away.

They hummed mirthful music;
they made lemonade.
They modeled some masks
for a moose masquerade.

They chomped on some crumpets with marmalade jam.

They put on some swimsuits
and swimmingly
swam.

"My moose are so marvelous!"
Martha declared.

Not much could match up
when her moose were compared.

So Martha,
quite merrily,
ordered one more…

and one more
and one more
as she'd done before!

The mailman delivered
her new moose midday.

She signed with an $\mathcal{M}$...
and they all marched away.

MOOSE
MAIL

3 Moose

$\mathcal{M}$

Sig. here

They munched macaroni;

$4 + 5$

$1 - 1 = 0$

$\div \frac{8}{2}$

they practiced some math.

They mixed up some mud pies
then jumped
in a
bath.

They baked homemade muffins
from morning
till noon.

They mamboed till midnight
by beams from the moon.

"My moose are so marvelous!"
Martha declared.

Not much could match up
when her moose were compared.

So Martha, quite merrily, ordered one more…

and one more

and one more

as she'd done before!

The mailman delivered her new moose midday.

She signed with an $M$...
and they all marched away.

"The more moose the merrier!"
Martha exclaimed.

There's much more to moose
than the catalog claimed.

Seems Martha was smitten—
what marvelous luck…

till one day

most all

of her moose

ran
amok!

They misplaced
her mittens!
They muddied her dress!
They used most of Martha's
shampoo, more or less!

They misused her markers!
They smashed Martha's mums!
They minced Martha's homework
and left only crumbs!

They messed with her marbles!
They tumbled her cake!

More moose were most certainly quite a mistake!

So Martha proclaimed that the moose must go back!
She wrapped up some muffins and helped them all pack.

The mailman arrived to collect them midday.

She signed with an M…

all but **one** marched away.

"My moose is so marvelous!" Martha declared.
Not much could match up…

when **her** moose
was compared.

For my incomparable mom and dad.
—LMB

For Jess, my marvelous, magical, magnificent moose.
—MC

Too Many Moose!
Written by Lisa M. Bakos
Cover and internal design © 2016 by Sourcebooks, Inc.
Text © 2016 by Lisa M. Bakos
Illustrations © 2016 Mark Chambers

The full color art was created digitally.

Published by Sourcebooks Jabberwocky, an imprint of Sourcebooks, Inc.
P.O. Box 4410, Naperville, Illinois 60567-4410
(630) 961-3900
Fax: (630) 961 2168
www.jabberwockykids.com

Library of Congress Cataloging-in-Publication Data

Names: Bakos, Lisa M., author. | Chambers, Mark, 1980- illustrator.
Title: Too many moose! / written by Lisa M. Bakos ; illustrated by Mark Chambers.
Description: Naperville, IL : Sourcebooks Jabberwocky, [2016] | Summary: "When Martha gets an unusual pet,
she's delighted by all of the fun things they do together. If one moose is this marvelous, then more moose must be
even better! Pretty soon, Martha has more moose than she can handle"--
Provided by publisher.
Identifiers: LCCN 2015032049 | (alk. paper)
Subjects: | CYAC: Stories in rhyme. | Moose as pets--Fiction. | Pets--Fiction.
Classification: LCC PZ8.3.B178 Mai 2016 | DDC [E]--dc23 LC record available at http://lccn.loc.gov/2015032049

Source of Production: Leo Paper, Heshan City, Guangdong Province, China
Date of Production: May 2016
Run Number: 5006036

Printed and bound in China.
LEO 10 9 8 7 6 5 4 3 2 1